The Sleepover Club

Have you been invited to all these sleepovers?

1. The Sleepover Club at Frankie's
2. The Sleepover Club at Lyndsey's
3. The Sleepover Club at Felicity's
4. The Sleepover Club at Rosie's
5. The Sleepover Club at Kenny's
6. Starring the Sleepover Club
7. The Sleepover Girls go Spice
8. The 24 Hour Sleepover Club
9. The Sleepover Club Sleeps Out
10. Happy Birthday, Sleepover Club
11. Sleepover Girls on Horseback
12. Sleepover in Spain
13. Sleepover on Friday 13th
14. Sleepover Girls at Camp
15. Sleepover Girls go Detective
16. Sleepover Girls go Designer
17. The Sleepover Club Surfs the Net
18. Sleepover Girls on Screen
19. Sleepover Girls and Friends
20. Sleepover Girls on the Catwalk
21. The Sleepover Club Goes for Goal!
22. Sleepover Girls go Babysitting
23. Sleepover Girls go Snowboarding
24. Happy New Year, Sleepover Club!
25. Sleepover Club 2000
26. We Love You Sleepover Club
27. Vive le Sleepover Club!
28. Sleepover Club Eggstravaganza
29. Emergency Sleepover
30. Sleepover Girls on the Range
31. The Sleepover Club Bridesmaids

32 Sleepover Girls See Stars
33 Sleepover Club Blitz
34 Sleepover Girls in the Ring
35 Sari Sleepover
36 Merry Christmas, Sleepover Club!
37 The Sleepover Club Down Under
38 Sleepover Girls Go Splash!
39 Sleepover Girls Go Karting

For W, an avid fan

The Sleepover Club ® is a
registered trademark of HarperCollins*Publishers* Ltd

First published in Great Britain by Collins in 2001
Collins is an imprint of HarperCollins*Publishers* Ltd
77-85 Fulham Palace Road, Hammersmith,
London, W6 8JB

The HarperCollins website address is
www.**fireandwater**.com

1 3 5 7 9 8 6 4 2

Text copyright © Ginny Deals 2001

Original series characters, plotlines
and settings © Rose Impey 1997

ISBN 0 00710630 0

Printed and bound in Great Britain by
Omnia Books Ltd,
Glasgow

Sleepover Girls Go Wild!

by Ginny Deals

Collins

An imprint of HarperCollinsPublishers

Sleepover Kit List

1. Sleeping bag
2. Pillow
3. Pyjamas or a nightdress
4. Slippers
5. Toothbrush, toothpaste, soap etc
6. Towel
7. Teddy
8. A creepy story
9. Food for a midnight feast:
   chocolate, crisps, sweets, biscuits.
   In fact anything you like to eat.
10. Torch
11. Hairbrush
12. Hair things like a bobble or hairband,
    if you need them
13. Clean knickers and socks
14. Change of clothes for the next day
15. Sleepover diary and membership card

CHAPTER ONE

Oh, hiya! I didn't hear you come in. Just hold on a sec, while I stick this sequin on… What do you think? What do you mean, what is it? It's a choker, you derr-brain. See? All the sequins and beads, with these silver ribbons to tie at the back? I'm making it for this party I might be going to at the weekend. Yeah, check my careful use of the word "might". It all depends on what mood Dad's in when I ask him about it. He's been mad for a week or so now, ever since—

Oops! Nearly gave the game away there! That's why you're here, isn't it? To hear all the latest Sleepover Club goss? Well, you've come to the right gal. I might be in a whole heap of trouble, but I've got some inside info on our latest disaster that's so secret, you've got to swear not to tell *a single soul*. Not even the other Sleepover Clubbers, OK? Even if they torture you by tickling your feet with grass stalks. This has to be *strictly* between you and me, or my dad will never let me out of the house again.

You probably know all about us by now, don't you? The Sleepover Club – five girls who really know how to get into trouble. Maybe you don't remember? I'll give you a quick run-down on us before I tell the story, then. But first of all, I've got a question for you.

Do you know that rhyme, "Five Little Piggies"? I know, it's a really weird question, but hey! My mates don't call me Spaceman for nothing! So, do you know it? "This little piggy went to market, this little piggy stayed at home, this little piggy had roast beef, this little piggy had none, and this little piggy went WEE WEE WEE all the way home"? I bet your mum or dad used to tell it to you when you were a little kid, maybe when you were getting out of the bath or something. And I bet they wiggled your toes when they did it, too. Parents can be so dorky sometimes.

Basically, my mates in the Sleepover Club are kind of like those pigs in the rhyme. Take me for instance. Francesca Theresa Thomas, known as Frankie. I'm probably the piggy who goes to market, 'cos I'm dead sociable – always the life and soul of the party. I like dressing up and going a bit crazy when I get the chance, to tell the truth. Mind you, I've calmed down a bit since my cute baby sister Izzy was born. A big sister has responsibilities, you know? I'm the leader of the Sleepover Club, I guess. At least, that's what the others would say – though they wouldn't say it in front of me.

Lyndz is probably the piggy who stays at home. She's the peacemaker, with a crazy family life. Lyndsey Marianne Collins is her full name, and she's got FOUR brothers – two older, two younger. Imagine that! Eight smelly socks on the landing every day! I don't think I could live with that. She'd love this piggy comparison, 'cos she's totally loony about animals of all shapes and sizes. She's particularly mad about horses, and spends most of her time down at the stables – when she's not hanging out with her best mates, of course.

The piggy with the roast beef would be Fliss, the girl with the best of everything. Felicity Diana Sidebotham, she used to be. What a cringe – I'd have died of embarrassment if I'd been stuck with a name like that! I know Thomas isn't anything special, but I'm well pleased I've got that and not Sidebotham. Well, she's not Sidebotham any more, you'll be pleased to know, 'cos her mum just got married. Guess what she is now? Proudlove! Not much better, is it? She doesn't have a great sense of humour, Fliss, so don't go winding her up about her name, will you? She lives with her mum and step-dad in a perfect little house with a perfect little bedroom and a perfect little wardrobe. She's a perfect little pain in the you-know-what sometimes, too, but basically she's a good laugh. She'd probably hate this pig comparison, though – she goes on and on about diets, which is totally stupid.

Rosie's probably best described as the piggy with none – but don't tell her that, 'cos she'll go mad. She gets really touchy about money. I don't think her mum has got much, not since her dad left home. But what's money got to do with anything? She's got loads of other things – a brother, a sister, a wicked sense of humour, a fab talent for singing and mimicking people, and four top mates. She's the newest member of the Sleepover Club – and we wouldn't have invited her to join if we didn't think she was cool.

Which leaves my best mate of mates – Laura "Kenny" McKenzie. We've known each other since we were little kids, and have done pretty much everything together ever since! She's the piggy who goes "WEE WEE WEE" all the way home, 'cos she's got so much energy. (Plus it's kind of funny, that bit about weeing.) Kenny loves playing footie and doing other sporty stuff, and is a total tomboy. Like, she refuses to wear skirts and dresses *ever*, which Prissy Flissy can't understand at all! Oh, except once, when she was a bridesmaid at Fliss's mum's wedding. Even then, she thought she looked like a meringue. Nope, Kenz would much rather be charging around in her Leicester City football strip and a pair of jeans. Kenny and frills just *so* don't go together.

So, ta-da! There you have us, the Sleepover Club, the fabbest group of mates in the world. We all hang round each other's houses at weekends and have sleepovers, which are totally *ace*. We have midnight feasts, and *reeeally* funny games, and play jokes on each other, and spook ourselves with ghost stories at midnight – you name it, we do it.

Oh yeah. Like I mentioned before, we also get into trouble. The major parental screaming fit kind of trouble. You know, when your mum or dad's eyes get so bulgy with rage you think they are going to pop out and hit the carpet. Well, this latest Sleepover Club adventure is no exception. If anything, it's totally WORSE than anything we've ever done before. So remember the pig rhyme (it's kind of relevant) and hold on to your knickers, 'cos there's a pretty wicked rollercoaster story coming up. Are you ready for it? You can flump down in that beanbag in the corner, if you like. Get comfy, get in the popcorn... and let's begin!

CHAPTER TWO

"Happy Birthday to you,
Squashed tomatoes and stew,
Bread and butter in the gutter,
Happy Birthday to you!"

We were all walking back from school on Friday, arm in arm right across the pavement – me, Kenny, Fliss, Rosie and Lyndz. And because it was my birthday that weekend, the others had all decided to caterwaul really loudly at me, and expect me to like it.

"Gee, thanks, you guys," I said, putting on a really cheesy accent. "Ah'm reeeally moved by your beeootiful singing voices— ow!"

"You're just an ungrateful pig, Frankie Thomas," grinned Kenny, bashing me in the ribs with her elbow again.

"Yes, I agree with Kenny," said Fliss in an exaggerated way, her eyelashes batting up and down like a pair of mad spiders. "We were trying our *best*, you know."

"I wasn't," said Rosie with a grin. "Anyone got any crisps?"

"LYNDZ!" we all chorused. Lyndz always had food in her bag.

"Hey, guys," said Lyndz, burrowing deep down in her manky old rucksack (it had a stain on one corner which Fliss swore was horse muck), "I can't wait for tomorrow, can you?"

"Why, what's happening tomorrow?" said Kenny in her most innocent voice, her eyebrows all crinkled and enquiring.

"Oh, you know!" spluttered Lyndz,

fishing out a squashed packet of crisps and passing them to Rosie. "Frankie's birthday treat!"

"Oh Lyndz, didn't anyone tell you?" said Rosie slyly. "Frankie's birthday treat has been cancelled. We're not going to Animal World tomorrow after all, are we Franks?"

"Give over," I said, giving Rosie a friendly shove. "Poor Lyndz has been looking forward to this for weeks, haven't you my leetle animal-loving friend?"

"Squeak," said Fliss solemnly.

"Oink," added Rosie.

"GrrrRRRRrrr!" roared Kenny, making us all jump.

"Yeah, yeah," grinned Lyndz, looking totally relieved. "Squeak and oink and grrr to you too. So it's still on then?"

"Of course it is, you great lummock!" I laughed. "Ever since Dad came up with the idea, it's been, like, *on*. He's even got the tickets!"

"Fantastic!" squealed Fliss.

"So I'll see you all tomorrow at nine,

then?" I said. "Round at mine?"

"Too right!" breathed Lyndz, in total ecstasy at the thought of all those animals she'd see tomorrow.

"Er..." said Kenny, consulting an imaginary diary. "Well, I'm not sure if I can fit you in between feeding Merlin my rat and winding up big sis Molly. But I'll see what I can do."

"OK – but when we get there, I'm not going anywhere near the snakes, right?" said Fliss. "Just so that's clear."

"It's clear," we all said together. It was only about the zillionth time Fliss had said it.

"Rendezvous-ing at oh-nine-hundred hours at the Thomas establishment," nodded Rosie. "Unless I have a spy mission to attend to first, of course. I take my career in the Secret Service very seriously, you know."

Saturday dawned bright and misty – a perfect April morning, with just a little breeze in the air. Today was the day we were going to Animal World, and today was my birthday!

I shot out of bed like my pyjamas were on fire, and hurtled down the stairs.

"Hey!" laughed Dad, swerving out of the way as I bombed off the third last step in a huge, flying leap. "Happy birthday, Frankie love!"

"Thanks, Dad!" I grinned. "What's for breakfast?"

Now, you might think I'm a total greedy-guts for asking that straight off, but it's a Thomas tradition that we ALWAYS have fab birthday breakfasts. Eggs, mushrooms, tomatoes, beans and veggie sausages for me – mmm! And Mum and Dad usually decorate the table too, with flowers and candles and, of course, PRESENTS piled round my plate. Coo-ell or what?

"Happy birthday, love!" Mum gave me a big sloppy kiss and a hug. "Would you like scrambled or fried eggs?"

Oh, man – birthdays are just the best,

you know? Eggs for breakfast, presents to open, totally being the centre of the universe to everyone you meet, and a birthday outing with your best friends to look forward to! I hugged myself secretly with a lovely little shiver, and tried not to think of the worst thing about birthdays – that when they are over, you have to wait another 364 days till the next one. Or even *365* days, if it's a leap year.

"One, two three, *Happy Birthday to you*..." warbled Dad.

Mum joined in, and even Izzy burbled a couple of notes and banged her spoon on the table, more or less in time. Pepsi barked hysterically the whole time. I don't reckon she thought much of Dad's singing voice, to tell the truth!

Breakfast was ace. Mum and Dad gave me a wicked watch with funky silver sparkles in the strap, the latest S Club 7 CD and a new pair of fantastic flared trousers with beads sewn all round the bottom. Gran gave me a little gold-edged book of proverbs – she loves proverbs, my gran. I got a really cool top from Pepsi with a groovy silver logo on the front, and Izzy gave me a baseball cap, some nice smelly soaps and a bottle of nail varnish with lots of teeny little glittery lovehearts floating in it.

I'd hardly got dressed (in my new flares) when the doorbell went for the first time. BING BONG! It was Lyndz – early, of course.

"Happy birthday, Frankie!" she said breathlessly, passing me a squashy parcel wrapped up in cute paper covered in tigers. "Are the others here yet?"

I looked at my new, sparkly watch. "Lyndz," I said patiently, "it's only quarter to nine. Give them a chance!"

Lyndz had given me a little purse made of shaggy blue fur. "I just thought it was kind of cuddly," she giggled. "You can get in some practice for all those animals you'll be cuddling at Animal World!"

By nine o'clock on the dot, all the others had arrived too. I got some really adorable little hairgrips from Fliss, a gorgeous woven friendship bracelet from Rosie, and some fart spray from Kenny.

"The fart spray would be really wicked if we sprayed it near the M&Ms in school one day," sniggered Kenny. The M&Ms are our worst enemies – and fart spray is too good for them, quite frankly.

"Now then, everyone ready?" asked Dad.

"Yeah!" we all chorused, Lyndz loudest of all.

"Then let's go!"

Animal World Wildlife Park was just the other side of Leicester, so it didn't take us long to get there. Mum had to stay at home with Izzy, so it was just Dad and us – and it was kind of squashed in the car! But there was loads to talk about, so the journey went really quickly.

"What shall we visit first?" Lyndz wanted to know.

We all peered at the leaflet Dad had got with the tickets.

"How about the spider house, Frankie?" suggested Kenny with a wicked grin.

"EEUW!" I screamed, and fainted dramatically on to Rosie's shoulder. Spiders are absolutely my worst thing, you know? I'm completely arachnophobic (good word, huh?).

"I bet you'd love the spiders, Lyndz," joked Kenny. "Tarantulas are really furry, I've heard."

"Well," I declared, sitting upright again, "you can totally count me out. I'd faint or something. Now, the bird house would be pretty good."

"Ooh, yes!" enthused Rosie, her cheeks getting all pink. "I've always wanted to fly!"

The rest of us fell about.

"You're not going to get a chance to fly, Rosie mate," said Kenny cheerily, "unless someone pushes you off the viewing balcony!"

"I don't mind what we see first," said Lyndz. "Everything's going to be totally amazing."

"So long as it's not—" Fliss began.

"THE SNAKES!" we all yelled.

"I dunno – I think the snakes will be pretty cool," said Kenny thoughtfully. "Do you think we'd catch feeding time?"

"Urrggh!" we all screeched.

"Girls," scolded Dad, "I'm trying to drive here!"

Lyndz shuddered and went a bit pale. "Well, I know snakes are animals and everything," she began, "but I don't think I could watch them eating."

"Snakes have to eat stuff alive," said Kenny with a gleam in her eye. "That would be well cool to watch."

Lyndz went totally white. "Seriously?"

Kenny shrugged. "Yeah, you know, so it's really fresh. Goats and pigs and things."

Lyndz swayed slightly in her seat, and looked really ill.

"Look, we're there!" I said hastily, to distract her. "Come on, everyone!"

And so we forgot about snakes' eating habits for a while. But boy, if we'd known what we'd started, we would have turned round and gone home then and there.

Animal World was all based around this one big house called Clifford Towers, with animal enclosures in the grounds and a teashop and gift shop. There were deer out in the fields around the house, and there was even a moat!

We ran around all morning like crazy. The apes in the Monkey House, swinging through trees on ropes and chattering among themselves were just like a bunch of old men. The otters in their pool, spinning around and swimming like Olympic champions were totally ACE. And the Bird House was full of the most incredible tweeting and whirring of brightly coloured wings – and I could understand how Rosie wanted to fly.

Now Dad had popped off to the gift shop to find a present for Mum, and we were left on our own in front of the Spider House, with *strict* instructions to meet him for lunch at one at the cafeteria.

"So," said Kenny, flexing her fingers with a wolfish grin. "Who's going in, then?"

"No WAY!" I said anxiously. "Not me."

"What if a million spiders were chasing you, would you go in then?" asked Rosie curiously. What a question!

"I don't suppose they'll be as bad as snakes," said Fliss reluctantly.

"Come on!" said Kenny. "Frankie, don't be such a wimp!"

"Yes, come on Frankie," coaxed Lyndz. "They'll be behind glass and everything, it'll be fine!"

I fixed everyone with a ferocious glare. "Not in a squillion YEARS," I said firmly.

Kenny started to cluck, ever so softly. "Cluck… cluck… cluck…"

"Kenny, don't start!" I warned her.

"Cluck… CLUCK!"

Arachnophobia or not, if there's one thing I can't stand, it's being called a chicken. I took the most HUMUNGOUS breath.

"OK, OK! Let's do it – fast!"

With a whoop, we all charged through the doors before I had a chance to change my mind.

Everything was very dark. Suddenly, I felt totally twitchy, thinking of all those beady little spider eyes watching me, all those horrible hairy legs flexing, ready to—

"AiEEEEEE!" I yelled. Something was tickling my neck! "THERE'S A TARANTULA ON ME!"

"WAAAAHH!" screamed the others.

And we all tumbled out of the other side of the Spider House as fast as our legs would carry us!

"Wha... what..." began Kenny, panting. Even she had got spooked!

"I... I..." I was having difficulty breathing, leaning against a bit of fencing. "I... felt it, I felt a spider on me!"

"Uurrrghh!" screeched Rosie and Lyndz, clutching each other and giggling hysterically.

"Er, where's Fliss?" said Kenny, getting her breath back.

We looked round at the Spider House.

"Do you think that spider got her?" said Lyndz fearfully.

We held our breath, imagining Fliss with a spider's fangs sunk into her neck – when out she strolled, like she had all the time in the world.

We gawped at her.

"What…" Even Kenny was having difficulty believing her eyes. "Fliss?"

I found my voice at last. "Fliss, why didn't you come running out with us all? Didn't you hear me scream?"

Fliss grinned, pink with delight. "Oh yes. I heard it. I never thought tickling the back of your neck would produce such amazing results, though!"

There was a moment of stunned silence – and then we all jumped on her.

CHAPTER THREE

"Man, that was a seriously good joke," said Kenny admiringly, as we lay back on the grass verge with our ice-creams. "Imagine old Flissy coming up with a joke like that! You even had me going there for a second."

"More than a second!" spluttered Lyndz. "Kenz, you were peeing your pants!"

"I'm pretty good at practical jokes, aren't I?" beamed Fliss. "There was this one time…"

And off she went, rambling on about an April Fool trick she'd pulled when she'd swapped the sugar for the salt at the breakfast table and made her little brother Callum cry. Oh-oh! It was never a good idea to congratulate Fliss on anything. One sniff of a compliment and she was OFF!

But good old Kenny came to the rescue, as only Kenny knows how.

"Yeah, well," she said, interrupting Fliss in the middle of her story. "Making a little kid cry isn't much to be proud of, is it?"

And Fliss shut up instantly. Re-SULT!

I hadn't been that impressed with Fliss's so-called "joke", to be honest. Well, how would you have felt if you thought your worst nightmare was coming true? And what if I'd had a heart condition?

Suddenly I had a wicked idea.

"So it's the Snake House next, is it?" I asked casually.

I watched Fliss's face with interest. I never knew a face could go from pink to green so fast.

"After all," I added, "as I went in the Spider House, the least you can do is go in the Snake House, Fliss."

Rosie caught on. "It's only fair, Fliss," she said. "You gave Frankie a serious fright in there. Maybe you should let her do the same to you!"

"Oh no!" squealed Fliss. "Not those horrible slimy things!"

I jumped to my feet. "Come on," I said coaxingly. "I'm not going to play a trick, honest. I just think we should see them, that's all."

Somehow, we got Fliss to the Snake House. And double somehow, we got her through the doors. There was loads of heavy tropical foliage in there, airy glass cages with plaques that read things like "Boa Constrictor, Brazil" and "Boomslang, East Africa" – and snakes coiled up in the branches. I didn't need to play a trick on Fliss. Just seeing her face was revenge enough!

Kenny fanned herself. "Blimey, it's hot in here, isn't it?"

"That's because the snakes need to keep warm," said a voice behind us. We swung round, to see a man with lots of curly brown hair grinning at us. His Animal World badge said "Jack", so I guess that was his name. "They are cold-blooded, you see."

"Cold-blooded and *murderous*," Rosie whispered naughtily in Fliss's ear.

Fliss looked like she was about to run for it. I *soooo* love Rosie!

"You mean like, evil?" asked Kenny, looking all keen at the idea.

"No!" Jack grinned, taking off his gloves. "Cold-blooded means they don't have an inside radiator like you guys. When they get cold, these snakes can freeze solid!"

"Best thing for them," muttered Fliss.

"What do you do here?" asked Lyndz shyly.

"I'm a snake handler," said Jack.

He sounded dead casual, but – man! What a scary job! I think we all gulped more than a teensy bit!

"You *handle* them?" gasped Fliss, taking a step back from him as if he was covered in gruesome snake slime.

Jack shrugged. "It's no big deal, honest," he said. "They aren't interested in eating me!"

Kenny looked enthusiastic. "What are they interested in eating, then? I heard they ate live animals."

Lyndz gasped and looked distressed, but Jack didn't notice.

"Yeah," he said cheerfully. "In their natural habitat, the big ones eat wild pigs and goats and things, when they can catch them. You'd be surprised! But we feed them more regularly on smaller mammals here, like rats and rabbits."

"Not rabbits!" said Lyndz furiously, stepping out from beside me. "That's horrible!"

Jack looked at Lyndz sympathetically. "Not to the snakes, it isn't," he said. "They need to eat, just like you and I do."

"But—" Lyndz started to say.

"Cool!" Kenny butted in, oblivious to how upset Lyndz was. "So do they eat them *reeeeally* slowly, or swallow them in one—"

"Kenny!" Rosie said sharply. Poor Lyndz looked like she was going to faint. "Stop asking such disgusting questions!"

"Hmph," muttered Kenny, looking disappointed. Then she cheered up again. "I heard we could handle a snake here. Is that true?"

"Yes!" grinned Jack. "Come back round three-ish, and you'll have a chance to handle old Hissing Horace!"

There was a strange, choking noise from Fliss, which we all cheerfully ignored.

"Hissing Horace?" asked Rosie.

"A tame python we have," explained Jack. "He's a real pussycat."

"He probably *eats* pussycats," muttered Lyndz.

I squeezed her arm, knowing she was thinking of her pet cats back at home, Truffle, Toffee and Fudge, and her gorgeous new kitten Zebedee. When I thought of Hissing Horace eating live animals, it kind of made me feel sick too. After all, I am a vegetarian.

Jack started walking away. "See you at three then, yeah?" he said. "Back here?"

"Sure!" cried Kenny. She then swung eagerly round to us. "Three o'clock, guys, and we could be holding a *snake*!"

Rosie shuddered. "Could be holding a *séance*, you mean! Kenz, what if it bites you?"

"It won't bite Kenny," I said. "She'd taste too bad."

"Cheers!" laughed Kenny. "And talking of tasting…"

"It's LUNCHTIME!" we all yelled together – and holding hands, we ran in a human chain all the way over to the cafeteria.

Kenny flopped down on the grass and gave a huge burp.

"Euw," said Fliss. "Kenny, you're disgusting."

"Hey, it was a good lunch, OK?" protested Kenny. "In some countries, it's rude not to burp after you've eaten."

We'd had a megatastic food fest in the

cafeteria. Fried mushrooms and loads of garlic mayo for me, chicken nuggets for the others, a massive bowl of gorgeous multi-coloured salad and CHIPS all round. And then, since it was my birthday, my dad shipped in chocolate cake for afters!

"So, what do you want to do this afternoon, then?" asked Dad. "It sounds like you've done practically everything!"

"Snake-handling at three," said Kenny at once.

Fliss groaned and hid her eyes. "Snakes, snakes, SNAKES!" she wailed. "Is that all you ever think of, Kenny?"

"Pets' Corner," said Lyndz hopefully. "You can cuddle lots of baby animals there!"

That sounded like it could be very cute. We all agreed we'd go there before the snake-handling.

Then Rosie sat up and pointed. "Hey, look over there, guys!"

We all looked round, to see a poster advertising face painting.

"That could be fun," agreed Dad.

"A bit babyish," I scoffed.

"Oh, I don't know, Frankie!" said Dad. "I quite fancy it myself."

Now *that* put a different light on things, because it gave me the most fantastic idea.

"OK," I said slowly. "I'm on for it, if you'll have your face painted too!"

Kenny laughed so much at the idea of my dad having his face painted that she did another massive fruity burp by mistake. Like, gross!

"Go on!" I wheedled. "You'd look really great, Dad!"

So would you believe it? He actually *did* it! I haven't laughed so much in ages! He went for this really cool skull in the end – well scary! I got painted like a robot, all silvery, with rivets down my cheeks. Kenz got done up like she was off to a Leicester City football match, so no surprises there – if it came down to choosing between saving the life of her best friend and saving the life of a Leicester City striker, there'd be no contest! Lyndz looked adorable as a stripey-faced tiger, Fliss was a pretty pink flower (barfsville) and Rosie ended up as a frog.

Anyway, before we knew it, it was two-thirty.

"What was that about snake-handling at three o'clock, Kenny?" Dad asked, admiring his black and white face in the face-painter's mirror for the gazillionth time.

So Kenny explained. Dad seemed really interested, actually. I reckon he was just as keen on the idea as Kenny.

"But let's go to Pets' Corner first," begged Lyndz.

"OK," said Dad, looking at his watch. "I'm going to wash this face off now. Imagine if one of my clients saw me! See you at the Snake House in half an hour?" And off he went, leaving us to head for Pets' Corner together.

Pets' Corner. Sounds pretty harmless, doesn't it? Yeah, that's what we thought too. But Pets' Corner was where all the trouble *reeeally* started.

I think Lyndz must have cuddled every single animal she could get her hands on at Pets' Corner. There were floppy-eared rabbits whose fur was so soft, you almost couldn't feel it when you stroked them. There were hilarious guinea-pigs with all their fur going the wrong way, and chattering parakeets, and soft white ducks with amazingly downy tummies, and fat golden hamsters... Talk about Old McDonald's Farm!

"Oh, they are so CUTE!" Lyndz kept saying, charging around from one pen to the other.

"Oh, they are so KEE-YOOT!" Kenny mimicked Lyndz's voice. "Come on, Lyndz – we're going to miss the snake-handling!" She kept looking at her watch, and hopping around like she had tin tacks in her trainers.

There was a funny scuffling behind us.

"Hey, check *that* out!" I pointed.

A very small, very fat piglet was standing in the middle of the path, staring at us.

"A piglet!" squealed Lyndz, sounding a bit like a piglet herself. "Let's see!"

Now, call me a pushover, but this little guy *was* pretty gorgeous. He wasn't pink like you'd expect. Instead, he was the colour of marmalade, with pricked little ears that kind of flopped over at the top. His tail was curled up really tightly, like a corkscrew or something. He stood there and waggled his little tail, and I swear, he *smiled* at us!

"Look, he's smiling!" cooed Lyndz, totally besotted.

"Pigs don't smile," pointed out Rosie.

"Yeah, and they don't fly either," added Kenny.

Fliss looked around. "Where do you think he's come from?"

I shrugged. "One of the petting pens, probably."

"No," Rosie frowned. "I'm sure it's just household animals in the petting pens, not pigs and stuff."

Lyndz was crouching down now, and holding out her hand to the little piglet. It wrinkled its nose at her and wagged its head a bit, like it was nodding.

"Funny colour for a pig," observed Kenny.

As if the piglet had suddenly decided to trust Lyndz, it trotted up and rested its snout in her palm.

Lyndz practically died with delight. "Look, he likes me!"

"He's probably after food," Rosie said. "Do you think he's hungry?"

"Nah," scoffed Kenny. "Look at how fat he is! Hissing Horace would probably like him for dinner."

Lyndz put an arm round the piglet and glared at Kenny. "Stop making such horrible remarks, Kenny. Pigs are dead intelligent – he can probably understand you!"

"What do you think he's called?" asked Fliss.

"Apple sauce," said Rosie wickedly.

"What about Sausage?" suggested Kenny.

Even Lyndz had to admit that was a pretty perfect name. So we christened him Sausage – a little orange Sausage with tiny trotters and a tail that just kept waggling like a disco-dancing worm.

"But where has he come from?" Fliss asked again, looking round her.

"I bet you he *is* Hissing Horace's dinner," said Kenny suddenly. "They've been fattening him up specially. He's obviously escaped! But they'll catch him, and then – SSLLLURRPP!"

CHAPTER FOUR

I swear, I thought we'd never calm Lyndz down. She burst into tears, and practically refused to come to the Snake House for the handling. Sausage wriggled so much that she had to let go of him – I didn't see where he went. I really could have punched Kenny for saying such a thing, when she knew that Lyndz was ultra-sensitive about it. I know Kenny's my best mate and all, but sometimes she can be really thoughtless.

"Look," I said, trying to smooth things over, "I'm sure that's not true, Lyndz. Come on, cheer up! We can ask the snake handler at the demonstration, if you like. And I bet you he'll laugh and tell you it's not true."

"Yes, come on, Lyndz," said Rosie kindly. "Why don't we do that?"

"And if it's true, we can register a complaint with the office or something," Fliss pointed out, which practically set Lyndz off again.

Even Kenny realised she'd gone a bit too far. "I was only teasing, Lyndz," she said with a shrug. "Don't get in such a razz!"

Dad was very sympathetic when we finally coaxed a weepy Lyndz to the Snake House, and he patted her on the shoulder a lot. The show hadn't started yet, so we hadn't missed anything. But about a minute after we got there, Hissing Horace made his appearance – and we forgot all about Lyndz. Which was kind of a mistake, as it turned out.

"Urrrgghhh!" squeaked Fliss, clutching my arm so tight, I swear she left her fingerprints on my *bones*.

"Wow," Rosie and I whispered.

Kenny was literally speechless. And that takes some doing!

You wouldn't BELIEVE how huge Hissing Horace was. His body was like a really thick branch, and he must have been nearly three metres long – that's practically twice as tall as any of us!

"Ladies and gentlemen," said Jack, grinning broadly. "This is Horace. He's a Burmese python, and he's full-grown, though some Burmese pythons have been known to grow to as much as eight metres long."

SERIOUS gulp. That was enormous! I could well believe that something that size would eat Sausage as a little tea-time snack!

Jack went on to tell us about Horace's natural habitat and how he'd been with Animal World for three years. Then, when he'd finished telling us the facts, he said, "So, would anyone like to stroke him?"

Dad stepped forward eagerly, and

stroked Horace on the head. We all held our breath. Visions of Dad getting bitten and swelling up like a balloon flitted through my brain. But Dad just turned and beamed at us.

"Hey, girls," he whispered. "This guy is really something! Come and feel him!"

So we did. We held him, too – and he was really heavy!

Fliss didn't touch him, of course. She refused to have anything to do with Hissing Horace – and she wouldn't even touch any of *us* after we'd handled him!

"I don't want to get snake slime all over my fingers, thank you very much," she sniffed.

And nothing in the world would convince her that Hissing Horace wasn't slimy. I bet you thought he'd be slimy too, didn't you? But he really wasn't. He felt smooth and warm, kind of like the bark of a tree, only with really neat, shiny scales. Stroking him, you forgot all the horrible stuff – like how in the wild, he would have squeezed his victims to death. He didn't seem particularly freaked at our painted faces either. I guess he was one chilled-out snake.

"It's just as well that none of us are painted like Sausage," joked Kenny. "Hissing Horace might try to eat us!"

I glared furiously at Kenny. That girl just didn't know when to stop!

"Don't listen to her, Lyndz," I started.

But… where was Lyndz?

I looked all around the Snake House, but there was no sign of her.

"Hey, have any of you guys seen Lyndz lately?" I asked.

Fliss, Kenny and Rosie all shook their heads.

"She probably went outside for some fresh air," suggested Dad, frowning. "She didn't seem all that keen on the snake, did she?"

We all walked out into the sunshine, and called for Lyndz. But she was nowhere to be seen.

"I think you really freaked her, Kenny," I scolded. "She could be anywhere now!"

Kenny looked kind of ashamed of herself. "She'll turn up," she said sulkily.

"Hey, we never asked the snake handler if Sausage was going to be Horace's dinner, did we?" said Rosie all of a sudden.

We all went very quiet. We should have asked Jack as soon as we'd got into the demonstration. Lyndz was still miserable, and it was all our fault.

Just as Dad was about to go off and report her as missing to the Animal World office, Lyndz showed up. Just like that.

"Hi, guys," she said quietly, clutching her bag tightly to her chest. "Is it time to go?" She sounded weird, kind of nervy and odd.

"Are you OK, Lyndz?" I asked.

"Look, I'm really sorry," Kenny blurted. Kenz isn't very good at admitting she's wrong. She must have been feeling pretty gruesome about it to apologise like that!

"No problem." Lyndz's voice sounded all

tight and tinny, like a Furby. It was definitely *odd*. "Is it time to go?" she asked again.

"Yes, it is," said Dad kindly. "Home for a birthday tea!"

And we all left Animal World, piled into the car, and headed home for birthday cake and surprises.

"Hey, welcome back!" greeted Mum cheerfully as we all came through the door, wiping our feet and peeling off our coats. "Come in, come in! Did you have a good day? I wish I'd been there, but…"

"It's OK, Mum," I said. I think Mum feels a bit guilty sometimes, about spending more time with Izzy than me. Well, Izzy is kind of little, so I guess she needs Mum a bit more than I do. "We missed you, but it's OK."

"We saw the most amazing snake, Helena," Dad started.

I glanced anxiously at Lyndz, at the mention of Hissing Horace. She was still holding on to her bag like grim death, and hadn't said a word all the way home. She couldn't *still* be upset about that Sausage business, could she?

"Tea!" announced Mum. "We've got crumpets, and cakes, and toast, and biscuits, and birthday cake, all waiting for you through here." And she headed into the kitchen.

"Psst, Frankie!"

It was Lyndz, tugging on my sleeve. She was looking *totally* weird now, with a really crazy glint in her eye. What was *with* her?

"*What?*" I said. "Lyndz, what is going on?"

"You've all got to come upstairs with me, now!" Lyndz begged. Without waiting for an answer, she started heading up to my bedroom.

"But the tea…" objected Rosie.

"Come on!"

The urgency in Lyndz's voice was unmistakable. We all followed her upstairs and into my bedroom.

"You're acting like you're crazy, Lyndz!" said Kenny irritably. "So what's the big hurry? There's a fantastic tea waiting downstairs, and my tummy doesn't want to wait!"

Lyndz's back was turned towards us. She seemed to be fiddling with her bag.

"Look, promise you won't get mad?" she began.

"Mad about *what*?" demanded Fliss.

"Well, I just couldn't leave him," whispered Lyndz, turning round.

There, sitting on my bed among all my teddies and waggling his little tail, sat Sausage.

CHAPTER FIVE

We all stared stupidly at Sausage, like we'd never seen a pig before.

"It's that pig," Kenny managed to say, after about forever and a half minutes.

"Well spotted, Kenz," I said, ultra-sarcastically.

"And he's on your *bed*!" said Fliss, in tones of total disgust.

"But what's he *doing* here?" Rosie managed to ask.

Lyndz had sat down on my bed, and was stroking Sausage's head so hard and fast it was like she was polishing him.

"I couldn't leave him there," she said fiercely. "I just couldn't. He'd have been eaten, and I would never have forgiven myself. *Never!*"

Kenny dragged her fingers through her hair, so it stuck up all over the place. "Lyndz, it was a joke! You know, a *joke*? Like we always play on each other?"

Lyndz shook her head so hard that she almost fell off the bed. "No, it wasn't. I saw the size of that snake. It didn't get that big on muesli, did it? You were totally right, Kenz. *Now* do you see why I had to take him?"

Sausage got bored of Lyndz's stroking, and wriggled out of her hands. With a *flump*, he slid off the bed – and started heading for the door!

My stomach did a major loop-the-loop at the thought of what my parents would say if they saw a pig on the landing.

"Rosie!" I said quickly. "Shut the door before he gets out!"

With a massive leap, Rosie flung herself

at the door, and whammed it shut. Sausage gave a grunt of disappointment, and Lyndz swooped down and tucked him under her arm like he was a swimming towel or something.

"Oh man," Kenny was saying, shaking her head like she had water in her ears. "Oh man UNITED."

"You know you can't keep him, Lyndz," said Fliss. "He's got to go back to Animal World. It's *stealing*!"

Lyndz just hugged Sausage even harder, and got this concrete-like frown on her face. I could see that persuading her was *not* going to be easy. And whose fault was that?

I whirled round to Kenny.

"Kenny, you are SUCH an idiot!" I hissed furiously. "See what you've done?"

"You are going to have to come up with some serious suggestions about how we're going to get out of this one, Kenz," Rosie declared, folding her arms and staring at Kenny very hard.

Fliss joined in with the staring, till Kenny really started wilting.

"Well?" I said, using the same voice that Dad always uses with me when I've been using his stapler and haven't put it back. "We're waiting."

"Girls!" Mum's hurt-sounding voice floated upstairs. "Where are you? Don't you want this lovely tea I've made for you all? Frankie?"

I made a split-second decision. "We'd better go downstairs and act normal. We'll deal with this after tea, OK? The last thing we want is the folks getting suspicious."

"And staying up here when there's a mega birthday tea downstairs is already looking *well* suspicious," pointed out Kenny. I think she was pretty relieved that the heat was off – for now, anyway.

"We're *not* giving Sausage back to those butchers," insisted Lyndz. "And nothing that you say will make me change my mind, so there."

I looked at my watch. "It's too late to do

anything about this now, anyway," I said wearily. "We can't keep him up here tonight – we'll have to smuggle him down to the shed after tea."

So we plonked Sausage in the middle of the floor, tied him to the bedpost with a pair of my tights, and shut the door, *very* firmly. Then we went downstairs.

I don't remember much about my birthday tea, to be honest. It was seriously hard, trying to act normal, when all the time, my brain was whizzing and fizzing and shouting "PIG!" at me. I guess the others were having the same trouble. Rosie spread Marmite on a piece of Mum's ginger cake, and Kenny dunked a piece of my lemon drizzle birthday cake into her tea for so long that it dropped into her mug with a spongy SQUOOSH. Fliss was trying bravely to chatter, but she told Dad the same story twice and her giggle sounded *well* nervous. And Lyndz didn't say or do anything at all.

We cleared everything away in silence.

I could see Mum and Dad looking at each other, trying to work out what was wrong. We were never this quiet – and we were certainly never this quiet after a major sugar binge like a birthday tea.

"Thanks for all this, Mum," I said, hoping that I sounded vaguely normal. "It was like, out there."

"Are you sure it was OK?" asked Mum slowly. "I didn't put salt in the cake, or spread the sandwiches with face cream, or anything?"

"It was all really delicious, Mrs T," said Kenny. "Honest."

"Yes, Mrs Thomas," added Fliss. "The chocolate cake was totally magic."

There hadn't been any chocolate cake. I gave Fliss a kick.

"Er, chocolate *biscuits*, I mean!" she stuttered. "The biscuits were, um, great."

Doh! You didn't have to be a genius to work out that we were up to something. And my parents were *lawyers*, so they figured stuff out seriously quickly.

"Frankie?" said Mum. "What's going on?"

She and Dad turned their laser-ray stares on to me. I couldn't lose my nerve now!

"Nothing!" I said, forcing a smile. "I guess we're just pretty tired after our day out. Can we go upstairs, please?"

"Already?" asked Dad in surprise. "What about all your usual games?"

"We're really exhausted, Mr Thomas," put in Rosie.

We all started yawning like maniacs.

"Well, I'd rather you didn't go upstairs just yet," said Mum with a frown. "I'm about to put Izzy to bed, and I don't want you disturbing her."

We gawped at her in dismay. But we had to deal with the Sausage situation like, *now*! The thought of what Sausage was probably doing to my best and most favourite only bedroom made me shudder. What if there was pig poo everywhere? When were we going to smuggle Sausage out and into the shed?

We trooped rather sadly into the sitting room, and plonked down on the sofa.

"Well, what shall we play?" asked Kenny, looking around.

"We aren't exactly in the mood for games, Kenny," hissed Fliss. "There's a pig in Frankie's bedroom, and we are in such trouble I can't even THINK about how much trouble we are in."

Lyndz had cheered up. I think she realised that at least we were keeping Sausage for the night, and that was pretty cool.

"What about Crazy Snap?" she suggested. "That would take our minds off things."

Crazy Snap was a cross between Snap and army training. You set up the furniture so it was a kind of assault course, with chairs to jump over and door frames to swing on. Then you played Snap until you got two matching cards. When you got the matching cards, the two players had to race round the assault course. The first person back who slammed their hand on the pile of cards won the round. It was well funny, and pretty knackering too – just the kind of game to use up any extra energy you had left at the end of the day.

But to be honest, there wasn't enough spare energy in my mates to run one short-life battery that night. We had a go, but after Rosie had banged her shin because she forgot to jump over the footstool by the door, and Fliss had shouted "PIG!" instead of "SNAP!", we gave up.

Mum was upstairs with Izzy and Dad was finishing something in his study, so at least we were on our own and could talk.

"Look, we'll have to smuggle Sausage down in the middle of the night," I suggested, as we drearily cleared away the mess of cards and furniture. "When my parents have gone to bed. What do you think?"

"I think my head's gonna explode," moaned Rosie.

"Izzy must be asleep by now," fretted Lyndz. "It's been *ages*."

But it was at least ten million years later when Mum finally came into the sitting room, to tell us we could go upstairs again.

"And whatever you are planning better be quiet, OK?" she warned us, as we jostled past her. "If any of you wake Izzy up, I swear I'll peg you upside down on the washing line."

Pepsi was sitting outside my door. She had that kind of alert expression that dogs sometimes get because they can hear the postman coming.

"Oh no!" I said, dismayed. "Pepsi can smell Sausage!"

Lyndz sniffed the air. "I can't smell anything."

"No, but Pepsi can. Look at her," I said unhappily.

She really did look like a dog on a mission. Her ears were pricked right forward, and her whole body was quivering.

"Get her away from the door!" hissed Kenny, looking over her shoulder for my mum. "Quick, before she starts barking!"

I grabbed Pepsi and ran downstairs with her, shutting her in the kitchen.

"Sorry," I whispered to her reproachful little face. "Hope you understand."

I decided that it would be a miracle if my parents didn't smell a serious rat any minute. But at least, unlike Pepsi, they wouldn't smell a *pig* in a million years. Maybe we'd get away with this?

Yeah, and pigs might fly!

CHAPTER SIX

"There's one over there!" Kenny pulled a dramatic face. "Poo alert, under the window!"

Even though the situation was totally drastic, I couldn't help giggling. We'd counted three poos and a puddle in my room so far, and Fliss was totally grossed out.

"Bagsy not me who gets rid of it," said Rosie quickly, bringing her feet up off the carpet.

Sausage oinked happily. He was sitting in

Lyndz's lap, like he didn't have a care in the world.

Lyndz rolled her eyes. "You guys are such *babies*!" she scorned. "Look, I'll do it."

Sausage was dumped into my arms, and Lyndz went in search of something to scoop up the mess. The best we could find was a plastic ring binder and a pencil tin, so Lyndz did this complicated flip thing and scooped everything up. Rosie checked that the corridor was clear, and Lyndz headed off for the bathroom.

Sausage *was* cute. He was totally covered in gingery bristles, kind of like Dad when he hasn't shaved – and his tail never stopped waggling! It wasn't long before we were passing him round the room for cuddles, though Fliss only stroked his nose while Rosie held him at a safe distance.

"There!" said Lyndz triumphantly, when she returned from her poo mission. "See why I had to take him? He's just too adorable to get eaten."

Which brought us back to square one.

We were never going to convince Lyndz that Sausage would be safe if we returned him to Animal World. So what were we going to do?

The first thing we had to do was hide him. Particularly when Mum stuck her head round the door.

"Everything all right, girls?" she asked, looking round the room suspiciously, like she was going to find some big chemistry experiment ready to explode in one corner.

Eeek! I just knew I'd be grounded till I was about eighteen if Mum saw Sausage! She gets pretty funny about hygiene, now we have Izzy in the house.

"Errr," I mumbled, shooting a desperate glance around the room.

Lyndz was quietly piling up teddies like a big cuddly wall in front of Sausage, who, fortunately, had decided to fall asleep on my bed.

"Fine, Mum, really," I managed to say.

Mum kept peering round the room, with a weird expression on her face. "Can you girls smell something?" she said.

"Manure," said Kenny promptly.

We all stared at Kenny in horror. What was she doing?!

Kenny pointed out of the window. "I noticed your neighbours spreading manure on their vegetable bed earlier, Mrs T," she said innocently. "I expect that's what you can smell."

Mum's face cleared. "Of course," she said. "That would explain it. For a minute, I thought..." But she didn't finish her sentence. She just looked at us all, long and hard, before shutting the door again.

"I can't keep this up," Fliss whimpered. "I'm going to blurt something out, I just know I am!"

Rosie took control of the situation. "Look, let's get ready for bed and then have our midnight feast, shall we?" she said, looking round at us all. "That'll give us something to do. Then we can set the alarm for Operation Sausage, get some sleep, and finally get this pig down into the shed."

We all agreed that this sounded like a good plan. So everyone bagged beds, jumped into their PJs and started a relay to the bathroom – always leaving someone behind to keep an eye on Sausage.

My room is perfect for sleepovers. There's my bed built into one side. Then there's the bunk beds, which are ace for when my mates come to stay. There's usually some kind of squabble about who gets the top bunk, because it's always cool being up higher than the others (though pretty scary if you have to climb down the ladder in the night!). There's loads of space for sleeping bags on the floor too. When we turn the lights out and turn our torches on, we can make wicked shadows on the walls and the ceiling, and spook ourselves half to death!

When everyone had been to the bathroom, we cut the lights, sat round in a circle on the floor and emptied our goodie bags for the midnight feast. Doritos and salsa dip, Wotsits, liquorice strings, marshmallow aliens, baby carrots (that was Fliss, being healthy), Dairy Milk and choc chip biccies – fabbo!

"Look, Sausage has woken up!" whispered Lyndz.

Sure enough, Sausage's little orange head was poking up over the teddies on my bed. He'd smelt the food!

"He's probably starving," I said. "We haven't fed him, have we?"

So Sausage was lifted down on to the floor, and we ended up giving him most of our food. He totally went for the carrots and the Doritos, and he thought the marshmallow aliens were delicious, too – but he couldn't figure out the liquorice strings at all.

Everyone went quiet, watching this little pig in the middle of us all. Somehow, I didn't think Doritos and marshmallows were a very good diet for a pig, but it was all we had. THEN…

We all leaped out of our skins when Pepsi started barking. *Really* started barking. Right outside my door!

"Someone must have let her out of the kitchen!" I said, my heart sinking. "Mum is going to go MAD – this'll wake Izzy up for sure!"

It was total action stations. I knew Mum would come into my room any second – and we had to hide Sausage, fast! But where? Now he was awake, it was going to be twice as hard!

"In the wardrobe!" yelled Kenny.

Lyndz scooped up Sausage and ran to the wardrobe. Woof, woof, woof! Pepsi was really going for it. We heard Mum running up the corridor – Lyndz managed to fling open the wardrobe door and put Sausage inside – and BANG! Our door flew open.

Pepsi rushed in, her tail a total blur and her nose pressed right down into the carpet. Somewhere down the corridor, I could dimly hear Izzy wailing, and Mum comforting her. And Dad stood at the door, silhouetted like a huge angry giant.

"What is going on in here, Frankie?" he demanded.

Pepsi was still going beserk, snuffling round the room and woofing in a deep, dark kind of voice. I managed to grab her collar, and hung on to her like my life depended on it. Which it kind of did.

"Nothing, Dad!" I protested. "We were just, er, having our midnight feast, you know?"

"Maybe Pepsi smelt the food," suggested Kenny.

Dad was totally unconvinced. After our weird behaviour at tea and now Pepsi, I knew that he wouldn't rest until he knew the real reason behind it all.

"Pepsi has smelled something, and I'm going to find out what it is," he said, taking a step into the room.

Sausage shuffled around inside the wardrobe. Pepsi broke into a fresh burst of barking. And I did the only thing I could think of.

"EEEEEEK!" I yelled. "A MOUSE!"

Rosie cottoned on. "Over there!" she shouted. "I saw it over there!"

Fliss burst into tears. If there's one thing she hates more than snakes, it's mice.

Pepsi shot out of my room and straight into the corridor. My plan had worked! She'd got totally confused and didn't know what she was barking about any more!

"Girls, girls!" implored Mum, cradling a shrieking Izzy and hurrying towards us down the corridor. "Stop this racket at once! At *once*, do you hear? What on *earth* is going on, Gwyn?"

Dad had managed to grab Pepsi, and was trying to stop her barking.

"The girls saw a mouse," he said helplessly. "Pepsi must have smelt it."

Mum glared at us all. "Honestly! Scared of a little mouse! And look at poor Izzy – she's terrified with all this racket! Go straight back to your room, and stop this nonsense immediately!"

Pepsi had finally stopped barking, although Izzy was howling louder than ever. Dad dragged Pepsi off downstairs, Mum rushed off with Izzy, and we were left alone.

We walked back to my room in silence. I reckon we were all thinking about what a close shave we'd just had.

Fliss wouldn't go into my room at first.

"What if the mouse is still there?" she asked fearfully.

"Fliss, you wombat, there IS no mouse!" I said. "Don't you get it? It's called a *diversion*."

"Derr!" said Lyndz, tapping the side of her head.

We all flopped straight into our sleeping bags, suddenly feeling so zonked that we could hardly move. It was like, we'd all been super-awake, and now that disaster had been avoided, all we wanted to do was SLEEP.

"I... can... hardly keep... my eyes open," said Kenny, in between the most gigantic yawns you've ever seen.

Rosie stretched sleepily. "Don't forget to..."

But whatever she was going to say, no one heard.

* * *

I found myself in the middle of the weirdest dream. Soggy marshmallow aliens were floating down from the sky, and landing on my face with a wet, flopping noise.

I opened my eyes, to see Sausage's shiny wet snout snuffling around my face.

In a flash, the whole of yesterday came flooding back to me. Animal World – Sausage – our plan to hide him in the shed! We'd forgotten to set the alarm!

"Hey!" I hissed. "Is anyone awake?"

Groaning noises spread out from everyone's sleeping bags.

I leant out of bed, and prodded the sleeping bag on the floor. "Hey, Kenny! Wake up!"

"Hmph?" Kenny sat upright, her hair looking like a bird's nest.

"We've got to go and hide Sausage in the shed!" I whispered. "Quick, wake up the others!"

Within moments, everyone was awake.

"Sausage must have got out of the

cupboard all by himself!" Lyndz was saying. "He's like Houdini! Maybe we should have called him Houdini?"

"What time is it?" whispered Fliss, rubbing her eyes.

I shot a quick glance at my rocket clock. Its luminous hands said ten to two.

"It's a perfect time, that's what!" I whispered back. "Come on, let's get this over with!"

We tiptoed out of my room in a long line. There were no lights on, and the darkness was pressing down on us like a big blanket. Gradually, our eyes got used to it, and we could see shapes. The banisters, the stairs, the hall.

"Coast's clear," I whispered, beckoning everyone behind me. "Lyndz, have you got hold of Sausage?"

"Yeah," she whispered back. "He's wriggling a bit, but..."

"Whatever you do, don't let go of him!" said Kenny. "And don't let him wake up Pepsi either!"

We stole down the stairs, past Dad's study, and into the kitchen. There was no sign of Pepsi, thank goodness – Dad must have shut her in his study for the night.

The moonlight made the garden look beautiful. Honestly, if you believed in fairies, you could just imagine them out there, having a groovy moonlight party.

"Kenny, grab Pepsi's lead, will you?" I whispered, pointing at the lead on top of the fridge. "We'll tie Sausage up with it. Dad's gardening coat is out in the shed – Sausage can use it for a bed."

"What about water, and food?" Kenny whispered back.

Rosie opened the fridge. There was some old salad and a bag of carrots in the bottom, which she grabbed. Fliss got a bowl and filled it with water. Then we gathered round the back door. So far, so good.

The door unlocked easily, but it squeaked like crazy.

"SSSSHH!" hissed Fliss, making much more noise than the door.

"Shhh yourself!" snapped Rosie.

And finally, we were in the garden. The grass was very cold and dewy – I don't think any of us had put on our shoes, in case we made a noise creeping through the house. My feet were wet and numb before we'd gone ten paces.

The shed loomed up like a huge haunted castle, black and scary-looking in the night. The shed door squeaked even worse than the kitchen door, and everyone held their breath – but there wasn't a sound from the house.

Lyndz fixed the lead round Sausage's neck, and Kenny and I took Dad's coat off its peg and made a bed with it. Rosie put down the food, and Fliss put down the water. Last of all, we tied Sausage's lead to a rake leaning against the shed wall, patted him on the head (Lyndz patted him about a hundred times), and returned to the house.

We'd done it! No one had woken up, and Sausage was safe – for now...

CHAPTER SEVEN

I woke up *reeeally* slowly the next morning, like I was swimming up from the bottom of some huge lagoon.

There was a *ssccrrrip* sound as the curtains were pulled right back. I opened one bleary eye, and saw Mum opening the window. Peering at the rocket clock, I realised that it was half past ten already! How come we'd slept so late?

"Come along everyone, wake up," said Mum, moving briskly around the room. "I've got better things to do today than chase you lot out of bed."

And she marched out of my room and into the corridor, with this look about her shoulders that said "don't mess with me". Uh-oh. I guessed she was still mad at us for waking up Izzy last night.

What else had we been doing last night? My half-asleep brain was trying to tell me something, but it had a whole lot of snooze layers to break through first. Then suddenly, I remembered…

"Sausage!" cried Lyndz, sitting bolt upright in her sleeping bag.

Mum stuck her head back round the door. "You'll be lucky," she said sharply. "Toast and marmalade, and that's your final offer." And off she stomped again.

Sausage! Sausage the piglet was still in the shed! Suddenly, everyone was wide awake, staring at each other. Last night was like a weird dream – and suddenly, here was reality.

"Any ideas on how to get out of this little problem this morning, oh Kenny 'Superbrain'

McKenzie?" I said sarcastically, wriggling into my jeans and brushing my hair at the same time (which is pretty difficult).

"We could tell your parents, Frankie," Fliss suggested nervously, fiddling with the folds of her top so they hung *just so*. Fliss really hates having to tell lies, so her suggestion was no great surprise.

"Yeah, right!" said Lyndz, as she packed her sleeping bag away with a determined *bash-bash-bash* kind of action. "Like they won't take Sausage straight back to his *death*!"

I hopped around the room, squeezing my feet into my trainers. "Look, let's go and have breakfast, OK?" I said wearily. "Then we'll have a proper conference back up here."

"Our parents are coming to get us at twelve," Rosie pointed out.

"Then we'll make it a *quick* conference," I snapped, heading out of my bedroom and down the stairs. I was totally sick of the whole business, to tell you the truth.

The others silently followed me down to the kitchen. I tell you, it was like a funeral procession or something. I mean, I know we aren't at our liveliest first thing in the morning, but this was like, *morgues*ville.

Anyway, it was just as well we were silent, because we overheard something which put a whole new light on the situation.

Mum was on the phone.

"... escaped, did you say?" she was asking someone on the other end, a small frown on her forehead. "On the local news? No, I haven't heard anything. You're right, the girls were there yesterday, yes..."

We all totally froze in the kitchen doorway, like we were playing musical statues.

"Ginger? Really?" Mum continued. "Sounds quite unusual. I suppose they'll be asking everyone who was at Animal World yesterday to go back there and help with their enquiries... And there's a reward? Oh, hold on a second, Janet..."

Mum was beckoning us into the kitchen. We moved forward blankly, like we had concrete boots on. I kept expecting the *durn-durn-DURN* music to strike up at any moment.

"I don't suppose any of you girls saw a small piglet yesterday?" Mum asked, cradling the phone receiver under her chin. "Only a rare one has escaped from Animal World, according to Janet down the road. They are offering a reward of a hundred pounds to the person who helps them find it."

"A what?" said Kenny.

"A p...p...p..." stuttered Fliss.

"Piglet?" finished Lyndz quickly. "Er..."

Rosie and I just shook our heads dumbly.

Mum waved us over to the breakfast table and carried on chatting. "No, it doesn't ring any bells here. It was only a few weeks old, you say? It'll be missing its mother then, poor little thing! Right you are then, Janet – see you later."

CLUNK went the receiver. CLUNK went

our hearts. Now what? This was a serious twist in proceedings.

"I think we should pay a little return visit to Animal World this afternoon, don't you, girls?" said Mum.

My heart stopped completely. Everyone else looked as panicked as I felt. Did she suspect? Did she, in fact, *know*? Mums can be telepathic like that, sometimes.

"To help with any enquiries, you know," continued Mum, turning her attention to the washing machine and pulling out sheets and socks. "Going back there might trigger a memory or two, which could help. What do you think?"

"Yeah, great idea, Mrs Thomas!" said Kenny suddenly. "We're on for that, aren't we guys?"

Fliss, Rosie, Lyndz and I all swivelled round to glare at Kenny. What was she thinking of? Did she want us to get into even *more* trouble?

One look at my best mate's face told me that she was up to something. She'd suddenly got this fiery look of excitement in her eyes – the kind of look Pepsi gets when we start rattling her lead before we take her for a walk. It could only mean one thing. Kenny had a plan!

I could see that the others had figured out the same thing. So we ate our breakfast as quickly as we could, and then sprinted upstairs like we didn't have a second to lose.

"Right, what's the plan, Kenz?" I said breathlessly as I slammed the door behind us.

"It better be good," warned Fliss.

Everyone looked expectantly at Kenny.

Kenny shrugged, and did a handstand up against the wall. "Who says I've got a plan?"

"Come on, Kenny, we've seen that look a million times!" begged Lyndz. "Tell us!"

"Tell us, or we'll tickle you to death," threatened Rosie.

Kenny came down from her handstand so slowly, I could have screamed! She loves spinning out stuff like this.

"Well," she said, looking round at our expectant faces. "We go back to Animal World, right?"

"We do?" said Rosie with a frown.

"And we take Sausage with us, right?" I said, suddenly realising what Kenny's plan was.

"Right!" said Kenny. "We smuggle Sausage back in, and let him go!"

"But—" began Lyndz.

"That snake won't eat him, Lyndz," said Fliss, suddenly figuring it out. "Frankie's mum said he was *rare*. They wouldn't feed a rare pig to a python, would they?"

Rosie gave a sudden whoop. "We're in the clear!"

"Not yet we're not," I cautioned. "We've still got to get Sausage out of the shed, into a bag, into the car and back to Animal World, haven't we?"

"Oh, don't be such a killjoy, Frankie!" Kenny scoffed. "You're just jealous 'cos you didn't think of it first!"

"Don't be stupid, Kenny," snapped Rosie. "It's your fault we got into this mess in the first place, so don't you forget that!"

"Humph," said Kenny, and did a sulky forward roll. She always hates it when she's in the wrong.

"OK, so we'll have to get Sausage out of the shed just before we leave, right?" I said.

Rosie tugged on my jumper.

"Then – yeah, I'll be with you in a sec, Rosie – then we'll put him back in Lyndz's bag," I continued.

"I'll do that," said Lyndz. "He trusts me."

Rosie tugged on my jumper again, only harder this time. "Er, Frankie…" she began.

"Just a second, Rosie," I said impatiently. "We're just getting to the complicated bit of the plan. So Lyndz puts Sausage in the bag, and she gets into the car last, so no one notices anything suspicious. Kenny, you— Rosie, stop pulling my sleeve, will you? Can't you wait a second or two?"

"That depends," said Rosie carefully.

"You've gone white!" said Fliss, looking concerned. "Are you OK?"

"Not really," said Rosie. Lifting her hand like some ghoulish kind of spook, she pointed slowly out of the window.

Like we were all in slow motion, we turned our heads to look out of the window.

The first thing I noticed was that the shed door was open. The second thing, and by FAR the most important thing, was that Sausage was happily snuffling his way through my dad's vegetable patch.

CHAPTER EIGHT

You know how they say your life flashes past your eyes just before you die? Well, I got some serious flashbacks of all the awful things we'd done in the past, and all the trouble we'd got into. But something told me that nothing, absolutely zilch zero *rien*, was going to compare to the trouble we were in now.

I don't think my feet touched the stairs. I literally flew down, sliding my hand down the banister for balance. The others zoomed after me, like it was some kind of

Formula One race. And *then*, to make things even *worse*, I suddenly remembered that Mum was about to put out the washing! Sausage was going to be discovered at any moment!

Swerving round the corner, I cannoned straight into Dad, coming out of his study.

"Whoa…" he began.

But then – bump, bump, bump – everyone else bumped straight into *me*. It was a miracle we didn't all end up in a heap on the floor, to be honest.

"Hey!" protested Dad angrily. "This is not a race track, Francesca! You are going dangerously fast – Izzy could have—"

"Sorrysorrysorry!" I said breathlessly. "Sorry Dad, got to rush!"

And I put on a final burst of speed into the kitchen.

Mum was just picking up the washing basket as we shot through the door. We gave her such a fright that she dropped the basket. There was a horrible clatter, and socks and pants and a few of Dad's shirts rolled out on to the floor.

"Girls!" said Mum furiously. "Whatever's got into you, stampeding into my kitchen like that?"

"Just got to go into the garden, Mum," I panted, trying to edge past her.

"Won't be long, Mrs T," said Kenny, trying to get round the other side of her.

But when Mum gets cross, she swells into a kind of elephant, and is *reeeally* tough to squeeze past.

"Just one second, young ladies..." she began.

Cue: my baby sister. When the washing basket hit the kitchen floor, iron-lungs Izzy had got a horrible fright. And – I don't know if you have baby brothers or sisters, but have you noticed the way they screw themselves up for a massive screaming fit? Their faces go red, their mouths get huge, and they go dead quiet as they suck in all the air they can manage. And then, oh boy. Then, they...

"WAAAAHH!" screeched Izzy.

Mum's attention was instantly diverted. "Shush, shush, shush!" she crooned, scooping up Izzy and cuddling her tight.

"*Now!*" hissed Kenny, shoving me towards the kitchen door.

"Run for it, Frankie!" whispered Rosie encouragingly.

But Mum swivelled round again and glared at us all, joggling a shrieking Izzy on her hip.

"Now look what you've done!" she snapped. "Is there no end to this disturbance? Your poor sister will be a bag of nerves when she grows up, Francesca."

I'm always in serious trouble when Mum calls me Francesca. And she hadn't even seen the pig in the garden yet.

Mum's next words nearly made me faint.

"I'm going to take Izzy out for a breath of fresh air and see if I can calm her down," said Mum severely. "When I come back in, I expect all that washing to be back in the basket, and you lot ready with the clothes pegs to hang it out. Do I make myself clear?"

"No!" squeaked Rosie, leaping for the kitchen door.

"I'll take her, Mrs Thomas," Fliss volunteered quickly, holding out her hands. "My mum says I'm ever so good with babies."

"Er, I think there's someone at the door, Mrs Thomas," said Lyndz hopefully.

But I could see that another Frankie stunt was required to get us out of this one. Oh well, here goes, I sighed. I was in plenty of trouble already, so what difference would one more little incident make?

"MOUSE!" I yelled.

OK, I know we'd done that one before. But it had worked last time, so...

Pepsi shot into the kitchen in a blur of black fur. I guess she recognised the word from the night before. Now we had Pepsi's barking, Izzy's howls *and* Mum's furious "Not *again*!"s to deal with. We all had to cover our ears, or we'd have gone deaf. It was crazy in there, even by Sleepover Club standards.

But it was worth it. This time, Lyndz managed to get past Mum and out into the garden. We were safe! Lyndz would catch Sausage, stick him back in the shed, and we'd be sorted!

Mum was pretty much speechless by the time we'd caught Pepsi and I'd confessed that I'd mistaken a bit of fluff in the corner for a mouse. She hadn't even noticed Lyndz slinking out of the kitchen door. Izzy had tired herself out so much that she suddenly fell asleep mid-scream. The silence was wonderful.

"Well!" Mum said at last, in a furious whisper. "I hope you're pleased with yourselves..."

Blah blah blah. By the time she'd finished "yelling" (she did it in a whisper so she didn't wake up Izzy again), Lyndz must've had time to take Sausage all the way back to Animal World. I didn't blame Mum, I suppose. We hadn't had this much noise since, ooh – the *last* sleepover round at mine.

"We're really sorry for all the trouble, Mrs Thomas," said Fliss. She sounded totally genuine, too. Poor old Fliss hates being yelled at.

Everyone nodded and mumbled "Sorry" a couple more times, just to be on the safe side.

"Hmm," said Mum.

"We'll put the washing out for you now, Mrs T," offered Kenny, scooping up the pants and socks and plonking them back in the basket. "Come on, you guys."

And we all tumbled outside with the washing. Phew! The garden smelled of freedom!

Lyndz was waiting for us. She didn't have good news.

"I can't find him," she told us anxiously.

"What do you mean, you can't find him?" I asked.

"He's not in the garden, Frankie!" said Lyndz. "Honestly, I've looked everywhere!"

I clapped my hands. "Action stations!" I said urgently. "We've got to find him fast!"

There wasn't much to my garden, but we turned everything upside down. I rummaged right to the back of Dad's shed. Lyndz wandered around, calling "Sausage!" in a hopeful sort of way, which was a bit dumb. Kenny waded through the bushes. She's quite good at that, since she's always in those bushes searching for tennis balls and frisbees when she comes round. Rosie wandered along the fence, jumping up and trying to peer into the neighbours' gardens. And Fliss got on with pegging out the washing, in case Mum was watching out of the window.

"Hey!" Kenny called out. "I think I've found something!"

She clambered out of the bushes and ran into the middle of the garden, where she managed to get all tangled up in the sheet Fliss was trying to hang out.

"Careful, Kenny!" Fliss said crossly. "I'm trying to get the ends of the sheet to match, and you barging into me like that doesn't help!"

"Oh, poo to that!" said Kenny rudely. "I think I've found some footprints!"

We all followed her back to the bushes. Sure enough, there were some small, pig-sized footprints there – but they were kind of hard to see, since Kenny had trampled all over them.

"Great," said Rosie bitterly. "What good's that?"

"Kenny's only trying to help," pointed out Lyndz. She's such a peacemaker, that girl.

"They seem to be heading that way," I said, pointing towards the house.

Towards the house?

Suddenly Pepsi started going totally mad. And we all heard Dad's voice as he roared across the garden:

"WHERE ON EARTH DID THIS PIG COME FROM?"

CHAPTER NINE

Needless to say, Dad went totally ballistic. Mum just shook her head and disappeared upstairs, leaving us in Dad's hands. I guess she didn't have any more energy to shout at us after what had happened earlier.

But nuclear war had nothing on Dad. We all sat in a row in his study and stared very hard at the floor while he paced around and yelled about "responsibility" and "idiots" and "I won't be able to hold my head up in public".

"Now, will somebody have the good

manners to look me in the eye and explain this?" Dad said at last.

The trouble with looking at Dad was that he had Sausage tucked under his arm. It made it kind of hard to meet his eye without getting the giggles, you see. And this was seriously *not* the time to get the giggles.

"Hic," hiccuped Lyndz suddenly. She always gets the hiccups at the *worst* times.

Still no one said anything. Well, we're the Sleepover Club, aren't we? We don't dob on our mates.

"Right, we are calling your parents," said Dad at last. "Let's see what they have to say about this. You lot, stay here."

And he marched out of the room. The last thing we saw before he closed the door was Sausage's little tail, waggling away under his arm.

Kenny started to laugh.

"Stop it, Kenz," I said sternly. "This is no laughing ma-ma…"

And then I got the giggles too. Soon we

were weeping with laughter, clinging on to each other like we were drowning.

"When your – your dad... hic! When he yelled, I thought my heart was going to stop!" giggled Lyndz, tears streaming down her face.

"Ouch!" groaned Rosie, holding her sides. "I'm in agony here! Stop laughing everyone, I can't take it!"

Fliss was the only one who wasn't laughing. "Well, I don't see anything funny about it," she said sadly. "We are probably going to be grounded for weeks and weeks, and we'll never be able to see each other again, and Andy was going to take me to the cinema next Saturday and that won't happen now. Mum will probably refuse to take me shopping on Saturday morning, too. Oh, how I wish we'd never laid eyes on that stupid pig!"

We stopped laughing pretty quickly when everyone's parents arrived. Fliss's mum wrung her hands a lot, although you could tell that her step-dad Andy thought it was pretty funny. Kenny's parents didn't look very surprised – with a daughter like Kenny, not much surprises them any more, I guess. Rosie's mum was very solemn and quietly spoken, but there was no doubt that she was pretty cross. And Lyndz's parents just talked quietly to each other, and shook their heads whenever they looked at us.

The questions poured over us like a tidal wave. Who had stolen the pig? Why? When? What had we been thinking of? What had we planned to do with it? But still no one said a word. I'm well proud of my mates, because it must have taken major guts. I think Lyndz was pretty grateful.

"Well, there's only one thing for it," said Dad in the end, shrugging his shoulders. "We'll all have to go back to Animal World this afternoon. You'll have to explain it to them there instead. If you persist in this silence, they'll probably call the police."

The police! I stared round at my mates.

What would happen? Would we go to jail?

"Honestly, I'll never be able to look my clients in the eye again after this," Dad went on. "The papers will probably get hold of it, and I'll be a laughing stock!"

Dad takes his reputation very seriously. He is a lawyer after all, so I guess his reputation is pretty important.

"Come on, Gwyn, there's no harm done," said Mr Collins. "Let's just get these little criminals and that piglet back down to Animal World. Everyone will forget about this whole business soon enough."

"What if they press charges?" wailed Fliss's mum. "I don't want my darling Felicity to have a criminal record!"

Fliss burst into tears.

"Don't cry, Fliss!" said Lyndz, practically in tears herself.

"Yeah, it'll be all right, honest," said Rosie, though she didn't seem too convinced.

"Will I have a criminal record too?" said Kenny, looking really interested.

"You be quiet, young lady," snapped Mrs McKenzie. "You're in quite enough trouble as it is."

We got out Pepsi's travelling box for Sausage's trip back to Animal World. It looks a bit like a picnic hamper, except with more breathing holes in it. Pepsi took one look at it and slunk off under the sofa. She knows it usually means a trip to the vet – so I guess she was pretty relieved when we put Sausage in it instead. Lyndz fussed around with a blanket and some carrots, and then Dad closed the box and stowed it in the back of the car.

"You'd better do the lid up tightly, Dad," I said in a small voice. "He's a real escape artist."

And twenty minutes later, we were all on the road, heading for our doom.

I was in Dad's car with Kenny and Dr McKenzie. Somehow, the journey took forever. I remembered how quick it had seemed when we'd all gone to Animal World for my birthday the day before. I could hardly believe it was only yesterday – it felt like a lifetime. I kept wanting to talk to Kenny, but every time I opened my mouth, Dad just glared at me in the car mirror. It was a deadly boring journey.

My heart jumped into my mouth when we finally swung through the gates of Animal World. Visions of gloomy police cells and clanging metal doors loomed in my mind. I've got an over-active imagination, Mum always says – and man, it was really working overtime.

"Enquiry Room?" said the guard on the gate. "Just park over there, sir, and follow the signs. You can't miss it. Hope you've got some good news about that little swine, if you'll pardon the joke!"

Dad muttered something, and swung away from the gate pretty quickly.

The others had got to the car park before us. Fliss and Rosie were with Andy and Rosie's mum – Fliss's mum had had to go home to look after the twins. Lyndz was standing quietly with her parents. No one was talking to each other – everyone just looked really nervous.

There really was no way out of this, I thought miserably. The Sleepover Club has gone belly up this time.

There were lots of people heading for the Enquiry Room. Apparently there was a reward, so I guess everyone was keen to help. I kept overhearing conversations that just made me feel worse and worse.

"Our Sarah saw that little piglet, she says – she reckoned it got through the fence and headed off into the woods."

"A fox will have got it, for sure."

"I think I saw it in our road, but it might have been a cat."

Dad was holding Pepsi's travelling box very firmly. No one seemed to have noticed that he was carrying it, as we were swept along in the crowd. Maybe everyone thought it was a picnic basket. I think Dad was kind of glad about that – his reputation, blah, blah, blah.

"Hurry up," said Andy, not unkindly, as

he saw us dawdling behind. "Let's get this over with, eh?"

"And then we can all go home," sighed Dr McKenzie, holding Kenny very firmly by the wrist.

"Hear, hear," said Rosie's mum and the Collinses.

When we got to the Enquiry Room, it was already busy. Everyone had to take a little number from a ticket machine, and sit down to wait their turn – even Dad, and he had the bloomin' pig! He tried to tell someone, but no one seemed interested. Duh.

At last, we could talk to each other – but we had to whisper.

"This is it, isn't it Franks?" said Kenny gloomily.

"We'll probably get fined, if not worse," declared Rosie. She definitely the biggest pessimist in the Sleepover Club, if not the whole of Cuddington.

"We might go to j-j-jail," sobbed Fliss, who hadn't really stopped snivelling since we arrived.

"At least I know Sausage will be safe," said Lyndz quietly. "That's something, I guess."

"Number 143!" called an attendant at the main enquiry desk.

"That's us," said Dad firmly, picking up the travelling box. "Come along."

My legs felt like they were rooted to the floor. Kenny tugged on my arm.

"Come on, Franks, let's do it!" she said.

"One for all and all for one," joked Lyndz feebly.

The walk to the enquiry desk took forever and a half. When we got there, Dad put the travelling box on the ground and turned to the woman behind the desk.

"So, what news do you have for us, sir?" asked the woman cheerily. "Anything useful?"

"Well," began Dad.

But he didn't get any further, because there was a sudden shout.

"Look!"

Sausage was standing on the far side of the room.

CHAPTER TEN

"It's the p-p-pig!" stammered Dad, totally astonished.

"Yes, I know you've come to help us find the pig," said the enquiry lady kindly. She obviously thought my dad was a bit mad. "That's what we're all here for, isn't it?"

"No, it's the PIG! Over there!" shouted Kenny.

This time, the enquiry lady looked. "Where?" she said with a frown.

Sausage had vanished again!

"He's under that table!" came a roar in

the far corner of the room. A man was pointing at a row of tables by the exit. "Catch him, somebody!"

I think the word "reward" zinged into everyone's head right at that moment. Because suddenly, there was a total scrum as every single person in the room started shouting, yelling and running. Dad was looking seriously spaced out. He kept staring from the travelling box to the scrum and back to the travelling box, like he was watching a game of ping pong or something.

"But how…" he started saying.

"Come on, guys!" shouted Lyndz. "He'll be scared, we've got to go and rescue him! He trusts us!"

"Yeah, go the Sleepover Club!" I roared, punching the air like I was mad or something. It was a pretty crazy feeling. I think all that tension had got into my head, and done something weird to my brain.

Lyndz and Kenny threw themselves into the crowd of people, all pushing and shoving to get hold of Sausage. Fliss jumped in after them, which was pretty amazing. She was wearing a pair of really thin-looking tights, and she must've known she'd get a ladder in them. Rosie and I tried to rush after them, but we got pushed back by the crowd.

"But how…" Dad said again.

"How indeed?" said Mr Collins, watching the chaos with a big grin on his face.

"It's a miracle," said Mrs Collins.

Both the Collinses were looking totally calm, like this kind of thing happened to them every day. Maybe having five kids does that to you? Andy and Dr McKenzie were just laughing their heads off.

"Did you shut the lid properly like I told you, Dad?" I asked, hopping up and down as I tried to see over the crowd.

"Of course I did!" snapped Dad. "I just don't understand it!"

"The piglet is famous for escaping round here, apparently," put in Rosie's mum. "I was just talking to one of the guards about it. He's called Houdini, you know. Rosie, what on earth are you doing?"

Rosie had scrambled up on to a chair, and was peering across the room. "I think I just saw Kenny," she said. "But there are a couple of other Leicester City shirts in the middle too, so I can't be sure."

I scrambled up beside her, and stared hard at the crowd. No one seemed to have caught Sausage yet, which was pretty amazing, since there must have been about fifty people and only one pig.

A sudden movement caught my eye. Just like magic, Sausage had appeared back where we'd first seen him! He looked like he was laughing at the crowd all struggling on the other side of the room. Honestly, if I hadn't known better, I would have said someone was doing a magic trick with mirrors.

I nudged Rosie. "He's over there now! Would you believe it?"

"Hey, and there's Lyndz!" said Rosie suddenly.

Lyndz was wriggling out of the crush, crawling through on her hands and knees. She must have seen Sausage make his move!

"Go, Lyndz!" I yelled. "Quick, go get him!"

Lyndz took a flying leap into the air, and WHUMPH! She landed right on the piglet, grabbing him round the middle. "I've got him!" she screamed triumphantly. "Look, I've got him!"

The room fell silent, as everyone looked up from the scrum. There stood Lyndz, all pink-faced and smiling, holding up the piglet for the world to see.

"Thank you all for coming," the guard was saying, as he ushered the crowds out of the Enquiry Room. "Yes, thank you for your time."

Everyone was shuffling out of the door and heading back to their cars. You could almost see the question marks bobbing in the air. Where had the piglet suddenly appeared from? What had happened? Had it really escaped in the first place?

"You can tell everyone's really narked," Kenny whispered to me. "They all thought they'd get the reward!"

We were all gathered together, waiting for the guards to finish clearing the room. Lyndz was still holding Sausage – or should I say Houdini? – and chatting happily to Rosie. And all the grown-ups were standing round Dad, trying to cheer him up. I didn't know what Dad was looking so gloomy about. As far as I could see, this totally let him off the hook – and us too, with any luck.

"Well, I guess Lyndz'll get the reward now, don't you?" I grinned, poking Kenny in the ribs.

"Ouch!" squeaked Kenny, rubbing her side.

"Oh, sorry, Kenz, did I hurt you?" I said anxiously.

"I think I saw someone tread on her in the crowd," put in Fliss, smoothing down her skirt.

I noticed with total amazement that Fliss's tights weren't laddered *at all*.

Fliss saw me staring. "Mum always tells me to keep a spare pair of tights in my bag," she said modestly. "You never know when you might need them."

"Hey, guys." Lyndz came up to us. "Anyone want to give Sausage a final cuddle? We've got to give him back in a minute."

"Are you OK about that, Lyndz?" I said. "I know you got really attached to him."

Lyndz shrugged. "He's going back to his mum. That's where he belongs, I suppose."

"What about the reward?" asked Rosie curiously. "Are you going to take it?"

"That would be totally dishonest!" said Fliss, looking really shocked. "I mean, you took him in the first place!"

Fliss had a point. We stood there and thought about the problem for a bit. And then Dad solved the problem for us.

"Right, time to confess," he said grimly. "Come along."

We all stared at him. What did he mean, confess?

"Don't think you are getting away with

this, girls," he continued. "You owe Animal World an explanation."

I couldn't believe it! We'd just got away with the perfect crime, and now Dad wanted to land us in it anyway!

"But Dad—" I started to say.

"No buts, Frankie!" said Dad. He had this really determined expression on his face. "You must all come along with me now. I think we should do this in private, don't you? The Animal World manager's office is just down the hall. We'll deliver that pig in person, and then clear up a few things."

We looked a pretty sorry sight, trailing behind Dad. The manager's door was looming closer and closer... Then it was so close that I could read the manager's name on the door plate – "R. Keating". I giggled at the thought of the Boyzone singer running Animal World.

Suddenly I had the strangest deja-vu. Keating? I knew that name from somewhere else as well...

Then it hit me. Totally simple. *Totally* brilliant.

I pulled Dad down to me and whispered something in his ear.

"Right, are we ready for the ordeal?" said Mr Collins with a grin.

"You'll all feel better in the long run," advised Andy. "Trust me."

"I'm sure Animal World will understand," said Rosie's mum. "Which is more than I do, to tell the truth," she added.

"Come on, Gwyn," said Dr McKenzie, buttoning up his coat. "Lead the way."

"Um," said Dad.

"Is there a problem, Gwyn?" asked Mrs Collins with a frown.

One of the guards came up to us. "Shall I take that little blighter, then?" he said with a grin.

"Lyndsey, give the piglet to the guard," said Dad. He'd gone a very strange colour, sort of blotchy red.

"But I thought you said—" began Lyndz.

Dad's face got redder. "Forget what I

said. Just hand it over, will you? Then we can go."

Forget it? Everyone stared.

"There is a reward, sir," said the guard with a smile. "Mr Keating the manager would be delighted to—"

"No, honestly, no need for a reward," said Dad. "Give it to charity or something." His face was verging on purple now. "Come on, everyone. Off we go, back home now."

Everyone was so surprised that they let Dad hustle them out of the door and into the car park.

All my mates started talking at once. They were absolutely *bursting* to know what I'd whispered to Dad.

"Frankie, what—" hissed Kenny.

"Tell us what you said, Frankie, or I'll have to kill you," Rosie threatened.

"Please put us out of our misery," Fliss pleaded.

"My lips are sealed," I said solemnly.

"Frankie, we're your mates!" begged

Lyndz. "I can't believe you'd be so mean not to tell us!"

"Listen," I said. "I made a pact, OK? You know about pacts – we make them all the time. And they mean silence *forever*, don't they?"

Everyone nodded reluctantly.

"Even under torture, right?" I continued.

Everyone nodded again, even more reluctantly. I think they could tell that I was serious.

"Well, whatever you said, mate, I owe you one," said Lyndz with a huge sigh. "I think you really just saved my life in there!"

"S'pose," said Rosie grumpily.

"At least we don't have a criminal record," said Fliss.

Kenny snorted. "Yeah, and I was really looking forward to that bit!"

I linked arms with Rosie and Kenny. "We should just be grateful that we've got out of it."

"Never look a gift horse in the mouth," added Lyndz.

"Well, you wouldn't do that anyway, would you mate?" I said cheerily. "Come on, let's go home."

Kenny didn't try to make me talk on the way home in the car. I think she knew she was on to a total loser. Dad didn't say a single word all the way home, either. So it was just Dr McKenzie making conversation. He kept saying things like, "Well, I'm sure you had your reasons, Gwyn", and then staring out of the window a lot.

Dad dropped Kenny and her dad off, and then drove me straight home. When we got in, he just said "Go to your room." Then he disappeared into the kitchen, where I could hear Mum moving around. It was Thomas Conference Time.

I didn't get as far as my room. I settled down on the stairs, to wait for news of my fate. Pepsi came to join me after about ten minutes, so we both sat there together, watching the hall clock. Tick tock, tick tock...

Mum stuck her head round the kitchen door. She had this strange, scrunched-up look on her face, which could have been either a frown or a really desperate attempt not to laugh.

"Frankie, will you come downstairs, please?"

Down I trotted, all obedient, with Pepsi following close behind.

Dad was waiting by the kitchen table. He cleared his throat.

"Frankie," he said. "Your mother and I have been talking. And I think we agree that you should be grounded for two weeks."

Two weeks? Hmm, not great – but not bad either, I decided. I waited to see what else Dad would say.

"We think you have probably learned your lesson," Dad continued hurriedly, "so let's consider this the end of the matter. I don't want to discuss it again."

And that was it! I wasn't totally banned from seeing my mates, I wasn't given any chores. Jammy or what?

You're dying to ask what I whispered to Dad back at Animal World, aren't you? Well, I know I told the others I swore a pact and everything, but to tell you the truth, I didn't. I just didn't want to tell them about this, because it's really pretty private. The Sleepover Club respects pacts, you see. Tell you what. Why don't we make a pact now? OK, repeat after me:

"From the top of the mountain to the bottom of the sea, I'll never tell a soul what you're gonna tell me!"

There. I can tell you now.

Remember I recognised Mr Keating's name? He's one of Dad's old clients – his name made me laugh then too, that's why it rang a bell. And you remember how Dad goes on and on about his reputation? Well, I just put two and two together. I pointed out Mr Keating's identity, and I said – come close now, I don't want anyone to overhear us – I said: "Dad, you're a lawyer. How's it going to look if you own up to pignapping in front of a client?"

I think Dad was grateful, in a furious kind of way.

There! I've finished my choker for the party. Do you like it? I'm going to creep *reeeallly* quietly down to Dad and ask him if I can go to the party now. The rest of my mates are going to be there – they got grounded, like me, but nothing too major. And I can't miss out on anything that includes the rest of the Sleepover Club, can I?

See you around!

Sleepover Girls Go Karting

It's thrills and spills for the Sleepover Club when they pack up their kit for a weekend of karting. But can they beat the awful Josh, track champion and son of the owner? Or will the mates lose the challenge and end up – shock, horror! – as Josh's cheerleaders?

Get out of the pit lane and speed on over!

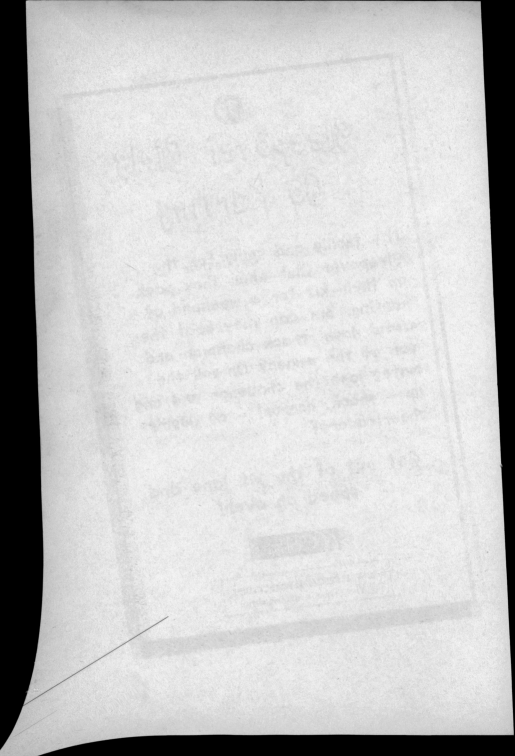

Sleepover Club at the Carnival

Carnival is coming to Cuddington! There'll be music, costumes, and even a part for Alfie the horse, if Lyndz has her way. Frankie and her mates do loads of research for their carnival float – and things get seriously interesting when they stumble on some old wartime photos of the village. Who's that girl, the one who looks exactly like Kenny? Is it coincidence, or could they be related?

Dress yourself up and groove on over!

www.fireandwater.com
Visit the book lover's website

42

Sleepover Club on the Beach

A long weekend of camping by the seaside offers a few surprises for the Sleepover Club. Their first surprise is that there are no funfairs or arcades near the campsite – boring! But then they find a mysterious message in a bottle, washed up by the tide...

Roll up your combats and paddle on over!

Order Form

To order direct from the publishers, just make a list of the titles you want and fill in the form below:

Name ....

Address ....

....

....

Send to: Dept 6, HarperCollins Publishers Ltd, Westerhill Road, Bishopbriggs, Glasgow G64 2QT.

Please enclose a cheque or postal order to the value of the cover price, plus:

UK & BFPO: Add £1.00 for the first book, and 25p per copy for each additional book ordered.

Overseas and Eire: Add £2.95 service charge. Books will be sent by surface mail but quotes for airmail despatch will be given on request.

A 24-hour telephone ordering service is available to holders of Visa, MasterCard, Amex or Switch cards on 0141- 772 2281.

Collins
An *Imprint of* HarperCollins*Publishers*